THIS

BOOK

BELONGS

TO _____

DISNEY'S
SMALL WORLD LIBRARY
THE
CASTLE GHOST
An Adventure in Great Britain

GROLIER ENTERPRISES INC.
DANBURY, CONNECTICUT

Developed by The Walt Disney Company in conjunction with Nancy Hall, Inc.
ISBN 0-7172-8211-2

"Here we are, Donald. This is Sir Reginald's family castle!" Mickey said happily. Mickey was looking forward to seeing his good friend Sir Reginald again.

Donald looked around. He had been glad when Mickey invited him to go to Great Britain. Donald had never been there before.

"Is this it?" asked Donald. "I thought you said this was an island, Mickey. Where are the palm trees? Where's the pool?"

"Oh, Donald, Great Britain is an island, but it's not a *tropical* island!" Mickey said with a laugh.

"Well, this vacation isn't what I thought it was going to be," said Donald as he stomped up the steps.

The big wooden door swung open, and there was Mickey's pal, Reginald.

"Jolly good to see you, old chap!" said Reginald. "So glad you could bring your friend along!"

Donald and Mickey followed as Reginald led them into the castle.

"Let's pop into the library," he said. "We'll have a spot of tea and get to know each other better."

Reginald asked Mickey all about his life in the United States, and Mickey asked Reginald what it was like to live in a British castle.

But as they talked, Reginald noticed that Donald was looking grumpy.

"What's troubling you, old chap?" he asked.

"This isn't exactly the island vacation I had in mind," said Donald. "I wanted to go surfing and diving . . . and swimming . . . and waterskiing, and get a suntan."

"But I dare say we do have some interesting things to do," said Reginald.

"What could be as interesting as surfing and diving and waterskiing?" Donald grumbled to Mickey as Reginald took them on the grand tour of the castle.

"Well, I say, what about having a look at the Tower of London? And there's also Buckingham Palace . . ." Reginald started to say.

"Ho-hum," said Donald, yawning from boredom. But Reginald misunderstood.

"I'm so sorry, chaps," he said. "I've been chatting away and you two have had such a very long trip—you're both probably very tired. I'll show you to your room. Maybe you'll feel differently after a good night's sleep, Donald."

In fact, Donald and Mickey were pretty tired from their trip. It was getting dark. Mickey and Donald unpacked their things and got ready for bed. As soon as their heads hit their pillows, both of them were fast asleep.

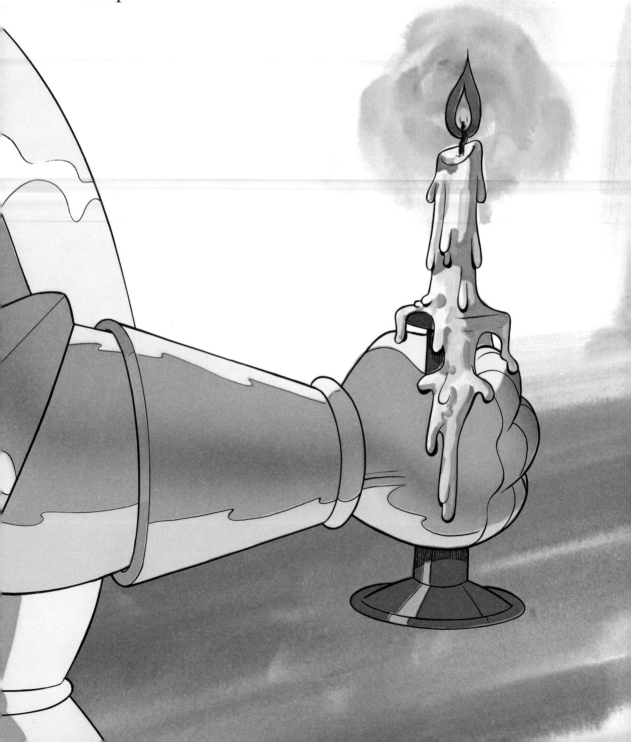

It was still dark when they heard a loud crash in their room. Mickey and Donald sat bolt upright in bed, staring.
    There, standing in the room with them, was a ghost! Dressed in an old suit of armor, it was weaving back and forth and carrying a flickering candle.

"I am the ghost of the gree-aa-aa-t Sir Chauncey . . ."
it said in a quavering voice. "And you are sleeping in my
roo-oom . . ."

"Oh, no!" gasped Donald. "It's a real live ghost!"

"If you wish to slee-ee-pp in this room," the ghost
went on, "there is something you must doo-oo-oo for me!"

"Ulp!" said Donald nervously. "Anything you say, sir."

"You must go on a quest!" said the ghost.

"A qu-qu-quest?" asked Mickey. "What is a quest?"

"What?" screeched the ghost. "You don't know what a quest is? That's ridiculous!"

"Just tell us, sir," gasped Donald. "We'll go on anything you want. Is a quest like a ride?"

"No, no, no!" said the ghost. "It's a search! You must go into London and bring back everything I tell you I want."

"No problem," Donald said anxiously. "Where do we have to go?"

"Oh—all over London," said the ghost. "And you must bring back a souvenir from each of these places . . . there are eight of them. I have a list here, all typed up. I typed the list myself, you know, on my good friend William Shakespeare's typewriter."

"Who's William Shakespeare?" Donald asked nervously, looking around for another ghost.

"Why, Shakespeare's one of the most famous storytellers in the history of Great Britain!" the ghost thundered.

"But . . ." Mickey began, looking puzzled and thoughtful at the same time.

"SILENCE!" the ghost declared. "Remember, I'll be back tomorrow night to collect my souvenirs!"

Then a gust of wind blew out the candle, and Donald and Mickey were left alone in the dark.

The next morning at breakfast, they told Sir Reginald all about the ghost in the night.

"Very odd," said Reginald. "I don't recall that we had a ghost in this castle . . . but anything is possible, I suppose."

"We have to leave immediately," said Donald, looking

worried. "We have to collect things from eight different places on this quest!"

"Would you like to come along?" asked Mickey, as they rose to go.

"Love to," said Reginald, "but I'm afraid I can't make it . . . too much work, you know!"

"Okay," said Mickey as they boarded a double-decker bus in London. "Our first stop is Trafalgar Square."

"What are we supposed to get there?" asked Donald.

"A pigeon feather," said Mickey, squinting at the list.

"A pigeon feather?" asked Donald, looking very upset. "We'll never be able to find a pigeon feather!"

But as luck would have it, there were so many pigeons in Trafalgar Square, it was a very easy thing to find.

As soon as they'd carefully put the feather away, Donald and Mickey walked toward the Thames River.

"What's next, Mickey?" Donald asked.

"Next we visit Westminster Abbey and Big Ben."

"Who's Big Ben?" Donald wanted to know.

"Big Ben is not a *who*," said Mickey. "It's a *what* . . . Big Ben is the most famous bell in the world! It makes the chimes for the clock tower in Parliament."

"Oh," said Donald respectfully, as he paid for their postcards. Then they headed for Westminster Abbey.

"Do you have everything we were supposed to get for the ghost?" asked Mickey as they stood on line to get inside Madame Tussaud's Wax Museum.

"Right here," said Donald. "All the ticket stubs and tons of postcards."

Once inside the museum, Donald and Mickey were amazed. There were wax statues of some of the most famous people in the world.

After the wax museum, it was time to take the boat tour along the Thames River, which wound all through London. The ride took them under all the bridges, including the Tower Bridge.

"Save that ticket stub!" Mickey said.

"Got it!" said Donald. "Now what?"

"Now we head for the Tower of London," Mickey answered.

"Oh, Mickey, I'm starving," said Donald. "Couldn't we stop and get something to eat?"

"Well, it just so happens that food is on our list," said Mickey. "See, right here, it says tea near the Tower . . . bring back tea sandwiches and biscuits."

But first Mickey and Donald looked at the Crown Jewels, the dungeons, and the armories.

"Now for food!" exclaimed Donald.

They ordered an extra serving so they'd have some to bring home to the ghost. But the tea and biscuits were so good, Donald wanted the biscuits on the ghost's plate, too.

"Oh, no!" said Mickey. "We're taking these home."

"Ridiculous," said Donald. "What does a ghost need with tea and biscuits, anyway? Ghosts don't eat!"

"That *is* true . . . " Mickey said thoughtfully. "But we ought to bring them back anyway, I guess."

Mickey and Donald took the underground train to Buckingham Palace. Buckingham Palace is where the Queen of England and her family live, and Donald stood outside the gate, hoping to catch a glimpse of them.

"I've never seen a royal family before," he said. "Do you think they might just walk by for a second?"

"I'm sure they would if they knew you were here,"
said Mickey laughing.

"What do we have to bring back for the ghost?"

"A picture of a Palace Guard," read Mickey.

"Well," said Donald. "Here come the Guards. I'll see
if I can get one of them to smile for the picture.

"Say cheese!" called Donald as he quickly ran up to
one of the guards and started to tell a joke and do a silly
dance. He never did get the guard to smile, but Mickey
got a great picture anyway.

"Boy, am I tired," said Donald when they got back to Reginald's castle.

"Me, too," said Mickey.

"Did you have a good time?" asked Reginald, following them into the library.

"As a matter of fact, I did," said Donald. "That ghost made us go all over, but I'm glad we did. London is a pretty exciting place!"

"Yes, it certainly is," said Reginald. "Funny thing, that ghost. Who did he say he was again?"

Donald shivered. "He said he was Sir Chauncey, and we were sleeping in his room."

"Never heard of him," said Reginald. "But I dare say you must be tired after being up all night with a ghost and then sightseeing all day. We'll have an early dinner."

As soon as the meal was over, Mickey and Donald went up to their room. But they didn't go to sleep right away.

"We have to wait up for the ghost," said Donald. "We'll give him his stuff, and then we'll get a good night's sleep!"

But they fell asleep in their chairs, waiting.

Just before dawn, a great crash made them leap right out of their seats. It was the ghost!

"Here are your souvenirs," Donald said when he'd caught his breath. "We got everything on the list, so now you can stop haunting us!"

The ghost started to shake and quiver, and then he pulled the helmet off his head!

"It's me, Reginald!" he said giggling. Donald was stunned. But Mickey started to laugh, too.

"What kind of a joke is this?" Donald sputtered.

Chuckling merrily, Reginald explained. "Best fun I've had in a long time! You see, I knew you could have a good time in London even though there isn't any waterskiing, or diving, or palm trees."

"Well, as a matter of fact I did," Donald admitted. Then he looked at Mickey. "But how come you don't seem surprised, Mickey?"

Mickey chuckled again. "Because I figured it out."

"How?" Donald and Reginald asked together.

"Easy," said Mickey. "When the ghost said he used Shakespeare's typewriter, I knew something was up. Typewriters hadn't been invented when Shakespeare wrote all his stories!"

"Oops!" said Reginald. "Guess I messed up!"

"Not at all," Mickey began. "We learned a lot about London . . . And we also learned that sometimes vacations work even better than we planned!"

"Not only that, I have all these great souvenirs to show everyone when I get home!" Donald told him happily.

Did You Know...?

Every country has many different customs and places that make it special. Some of the things that make Great Britain special are mentioned below. Do you recognize any of them from the story?

At Westminster Abbey, English kings and queens have been crowned for nearly one thousand years.

The Tower of London has been a fort, a palace, and a prison in the past. Today it is a museum. It contains the Crown Jewels and other treasures belonging to the royal family.

London's famous double-decker buses carry 145,000 people to work every day. The bus drivers need special training to drive these unusual buses.

Big Ben is the name of the giant-sized bell inside the clock tower of London's Houses of Parliament. The bell weighs 12 tons, and it was named after Sir Benjamin Hall, a city official who was also called "Big Ben."

At Madame Tussaud's famous wax museum, all the statues are made of wax—and they look surprisingly real. Even Donald has trouble deciding which Mickey is which.

Buckingham Palace has been the official London home of the British royal family for over 150 years. When the flag is flying over the palace, it means the Queen is home. Being a guard at the palace is a very serious job, and the guards are not allowed to speak or smile while on duty.

Four o'clock is tea time in Great Britain. Tea is often served along with small sandwiches made with cucumbers, radishes, or delicious spreads. Small pastries and raisin biscuits (called scones and eaten with fresh whipped cream and jellies), are also served. Donald definitely thinks tea time is a wonderful idea.

Most castles found in Great Britain are museums today. British people usually live in smaller houses or apartments called "flats."